Five Grr-ific Tales!

Ready-to-Read

Simon Spotlight
New York   London   Toronto   Sydney   New Delhi

Includes:

Friends Forever!
Daniel Goes Camping!
Clean-Up Time!
Daniel Visits the Library
Baking Day!

SIMON SPOTLIGHT
An imprint of Simon & Schuster Children's Publishing Division
1230 Avenue of the Americas, New York, New York 10020
This Simon Spotlight paperback edition May 2024
Friends Forever! © 2022 The Fred Rogers Company; adapted by Natalie Shaw;
poses and layouts by Jason Fruchter
Daniel Goes Camping! © 2020 The Fred Rogers Company; adapted by May Nakamura;
based on the screenplay "The Family Campout" written by Becky Friedman;
poses and layouts by Jason Fruchter
Clean-Up Time! © 2020 The Fred Rogers Company; adapted by Patty Michaels; based on
the screenplays by Mary Jacobson and Monique D. Hall;
poses and layouts by Jason Fruchter
Daniel Visits the Library © 2015 The Fred Rogers Company; adapted by Maggie Testa;
based on the screenplay "Calm for Storytime" written by Wendy Harris;
poses and layouts by Jason Fruchter
Baking Day! © 2021 The Fred Rogers Company; adapted by Natalie Shaw; based on the
screenplay "Baking Mistakes" written by Becky Friedman;
poses and layouts by Jason Fruchter

Simon & Schuster: Celebrating 100 Years of Publishing in 2024
For information about special discounts for bulk purchases, please contact
Simon & Schuster Special Sales at 1-866-506-1949 or business@simonandschuster.com.
Manufactured in China 0124 SCP
2 4 6 8 10 9 7 5 3 1
ISBN 978-1-6659-5945-2 (pbk)
ISBN 978-1-5344-9898-3 (*Friends Forever!* ebook)
ISBN 978-1-5344-6425-4 (*Daniel Goes Camping!* ebook)
ISBN 978-1-5344-7988-3 (*Clean-Up Time!* ebook)
ISBN 978-1-4814-4174-2 (*Daniel Visits the Library* ebook)
ISBN 978-1-5344-9509-8 (*Baking Day!* ebook)
These titles were previously published individually by Simon Spotlight
with slightly different text and art.

Friends Forever!

Daniel Tiger is
at school.

"Prince Wednesday is playing with Jodi. He is too busy to race cars," Daniel says.

Teacher Harriet sings, ♪ "Even when friends play with someone new, they will still be friends with you." ♪ ♪

"We are still friends, Daniel, and now we are ready to race!" Prince Wednesday says.

Then Jodi and Daniel pretend they are moving to a new house.

O the Owl wants to look at books with Daniel.

"I am playing with Jodi now, but I can play with you after," says Daniel.

"We are friends," says Daniel. "I will always be your friend!"

Daniel has an idea and says, "We need books for our new house too."

Daniel Goes Camping!

Hi, neighbor! Today

I am going camping!

I pack my sleeping bag. Dad packs the tent and the food.

Katerina, Prince Wednesday, and Miss Elaina are camping too!

The tent is like
a cozy little house.

Katerina finds an acorn.

Prince Wednesday does not find a treasure.

"We can help you look," we say.

Music Man Stan

plays his guitar.

Clean-Up Time!

Hi, neighbor! Today Katerina and I are going on a picnic.

We are going
to have our picnic
at the playground!

We ride Trolley
to the playground.

My mom and dad come with us.

Oh no!

The playground is covered with garbage!

Dad says the wind must have caused the mess.

King Friday goes to the playground. He asks everyone to help clean up.

It is important to keep our neighborhood clean.

We each get a pair of gloves and bags to put the garbage in.

We will all work together!

We can play after we clean up the playground.

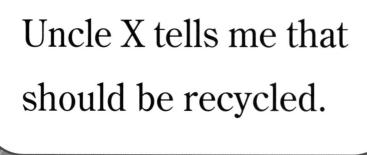

Uncle X tells me that should be recycled.

To recycle means to turn something old into something new!

Then O the Owl shows me a book about how to recycle.

Katerina does not
want to help clean up.
She wants to play.

When we all clean together, we can make a big difference in our neighborhood!

Miss Elaina comes over
to help us.

We do a great job cleaning up together!

Then it is time to play!

Daniel Visits the Library

Hi, neighbor!

We are going to the

library for storytime.

X the Owl reads a book to us.

Prince Wednesday hops like a frog.

"Ribbit, ribbit," he says.

"Storytime is a time to be quiet and calm," says X the Owl.

Do you know how we can help Prince Wednesday feel calm?

We listen to the story.

X the Owl finishes the story.

"The end," he says.

Have you ever wanted to be calm when you were excited?

Baking Day!

Daniel Tiger and Prince Tuesday are helping Baker Aker today.

Baker Aker has a recipe.

Prince Wednesday starts to dance as he adds the sugar.

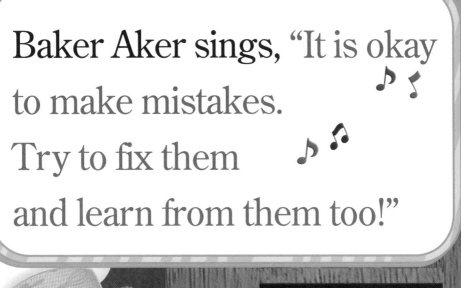

Baker Aker sings, "It is okay to make mistakes. Try to fix them and learn from them too!"

Prince Wednesday
cleans up
while Daniel gets
more milk.

Soon they have dough!
They roll it out.

Baker Aker gives them
cookie cutters
shaped like trolleys.

They make the cookies
and place them
on a baking sheet.

"You can mix it back in with your dough to make a new cookie," Baker Aker says.

After they are baked,
the cookies have to cool.

Decorate your own Cookies!

Hi, neighbor! Do you like baking cookies at home? One of the best parts of making cookies is decorating them! Ask a grown-up for help and decorate your cookies to look just like me, Daniel Tiger! All you need to do is add colorful stripes and whiskers to round cookies.

Ugga Mugga!